... ...

... f... ...ying will become s...ething
you can enjoy together!

My hope is that this timeless story about
friendship will inspire you not only to tidy,
but also to discover its transformational
magic as a family.

Sincerely,

Marie Kondo

For Takumi and our beautiful daughters . . .
who spark joy for me every day —M.K.

For Chris, Max, and Mason, with love —S.Y.

ned in the USA 2019 by Crown Books for Young Readers
First published in the UK 2019 by Macmillan Children's Books
an imprint of Pan Macmillan
The Smithson, 6 Briset Street, London, EC1M 5NR
Associated companies throughout the world
www.panmacmillan.com

ISBN: 9781529032116

1 3 5 7 9 8 6 4 2

A CIP catalogue record for this book is available from
the British Library.

Printed in Poland

Kiki & Jax

the life-changing magic of friendship

marie kondo

co-written and illustrated by salina yoon

Macmillan Children's Books

Kiki and Jax were best friends.

But they didn't always like doing things the same way.

Jax enjoyed sorting, and Kiki enjoyed collecting.

Kiki's collection of things grew and grew
until she ran out of places to put them.

So she packed her pine cones under the bed . . .

. . . stashed her nuts under the rug,

and piled her clothes in the bath.

When Jax came over, he asked,
"Do you want to play football?"

"Sorry," replied Kiki. "I lost my ball."

So Jax went home.

The next day, Jax asked,
"Do you want to go swimming?"

"Sure! Let me get my swimsuit!" said Kiki.

Kiki searched her drawers,

her wardrobe,

and even her toy box,
but she couldn't find it anywhere.

So Jax went home.

He missed Kiki. But *things* got in the way.

"Maybe Kiki forgot we're friends," thought Jax.
So he made something special to remind her.

He put it in a box to take to her the next day.

KNOCK! KNOCK!
KNOCK! KNOCK!

Jax knocked and knocked.
And waited and waited.

To Kiki, getting to the front door felt
like running an obstacle course!

By the time Kiki reached the door, Jax was gone.
But he had left her a package.

"A friendship scrapbook!" exclaimed Kiki.

It filled her heart until she could hardly breathe.

So she took a deep breath and ran to Jax's house.

"I missed you, Jax!" said Kiki. "Can we play here?"
"Sure!" said Jax.

They pulled out their . . .

favourite games

ROAR!

and costumes,

and looked at their friendship
scrapbook together.

After they finished playing,
Jax put the games and costumes away.

"I wish we could play at my house, too," said Kiki.
"But there's just no room!"

"Yes there IS!" said Jax. "Let me show you!"

Jax was excited. Kiki was overwhelmed.

"Let's play **PILES.** You make piles of similar items. Then, you can decide what to keep," said Jax.

They made a pile for clothes,

books,

and toys.

"If it sparks joy in your heart," Jax said, "keep it!
And if it doesn't, thank it and let it go."

Kiki and Jax sorted all of the items into boxes for keeping, donating, recycling, and throwing away.

Jax taught Kiki how to fold her clothes

and put them upright in her drawers.

Now Kiki could find a place for things that mattered most, like her favourite books, extra-bubbly bubble baths . . .

and most important . . .

. . . room for her best friend, Jax.

How to Fold a Shirt
the KonMari Way

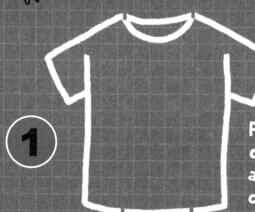

1

Fold one side of the shirt across the centre.

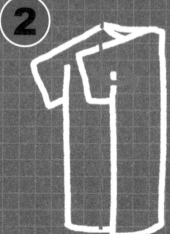

2

Fold back the sleeve.

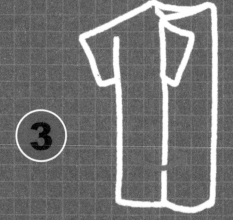

3

Fold the other side of the shirt across the centre.

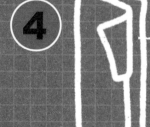

4

Stop a little before the edge.

Then fold back the sleeve.